Raincoats AND Rainbows

Elizabeth Redhead Kriston, CCC-SLP
Illustrated by Gary Morgan

Read with Me!® Strategies for Raincoats and Rainbows
Friendly Questions~Predicting~Echo Reading

National Reading Panel Skills Targeted
Vocabulary ~ Phonemic Awareness

Raincoats and Rainbows
By Elizabeth Redhead Kriston

Illustrated by Gary Morgan

ISBN   978-0-9909697-1-6

Cover by Melissa Clark

Layout by Melissa Clark

Printed in the United States of America

READ WITH ME PRESS
www.readwme.com

A division of:
Dynamic Resources, LLC
5306 Tanoma Road
Indiana, PA 15701
www.dynamic-resources.org

For Madeline and Makena who maintain a joyful and innocent appreciation for the simple things in life.

-Elizabeth Redhead Kriston

What do you like about rainy days?

Raincoats and rainbows.

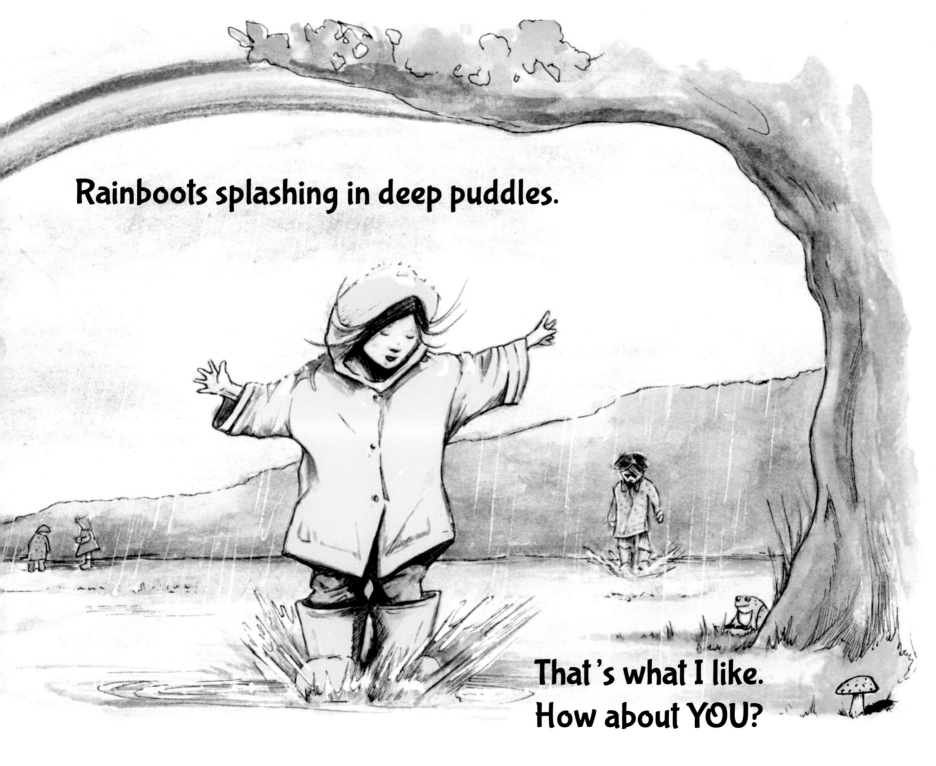

What do you like about sunny days?

Swimsuits and swimming pools.

Popsicles dribbling down my chin.

That's what I like.
How about YOU?

What do you like about snowy days?

Snowsuits and snowflakes.

Sleds flying over snowbanks.

That's what I like.
How about YOU?

What do you like about foggy days?

Pjs and pizza.

Building forts out of furniture and sheets.

That's what I like.
How about YOU?

What do you like about icy days?

Sweaters and soup.

Skating down sidewalks in my boots.

That's what I like.
How about YOU?

What do you like about windy days?

Jackets and jumpropes.

Kites dancing in the cloudless sky.

That's what I like.
How about YOU?

What do you like about school days?

Backpacks and busses.

Learning to write my name all by myself.

That's what I like.
How about YOU?

What do you like about Saturdays?

Playclothes and parks.

Playing with mommy and daddy all day long.

That's what I like.
How about YOU?

Do you like these things, too?

ABOUT THE AUTHOR

Elizabeth Redhead Kriston is a mother of two and an ASHA certified speech-language pathologist with years of experience helping young children build their language, speech, and pre-reading skills. Elizabeth's love of children and literature inspired her to write children's books.

You can find more of her books at: *www.dynamic-resources.org*

ABOUT THE ILLUSTRATOR

Gary Morgan is an artist living in Pittsburgh, Pennslyvania. Fantasy and horror genres are his main concentration, but he appreciates most art and has a new-found love of children's book illustrations. He spends his days creating artwork and taking care of his four-year-old son.

For more of Gary's art visit: *www.gmorganart.com*

MORE BOOKS TO BUILD STRONG TALKING, LISTENING, AND READING SKILLS FROM DYNAMIC RESOURCES/READ WITH ME PRESS

By Elizabeth Redhead Kriston

The Bark Park (voicing)
Go By Goat (final consonant deletion)
Pants on Ants (initial consonant deletion)
Sail by a Tail (stopping)

By Shari Robertson

Capering Cows (echo and paired reading/vocabulary)
Shivering Sheep (echo and paired reading/prediction)
My Cow Can Bow (front/back contrasts)

By Peggy Agee

Run, Turkey, Run! (echo reading, reader's theatre, prepositions)
The Adventures of Sadie and Sam (verb tenses)

By Suzy Lederer

I Can Do That! (early verbs and gestures)
I Can Play That! (reader's theatre)

By Alexandra Crouse

Spotless Spot (wordless books)

www.dynamic-resources.org AND *www.readwme.com*

How to Use this Book

Raincoats and Rainbows includes friendly questions that are built right into the story to encourage children to participate during the reading interaction, engage in critical thinking, and use more complex language.

Here's how you can help your child build key language and literacy skills and a life-long love of reading.

Use the open-ended "FRIENDLY QUESTIONS" *(What do you like about....?)* to help your child become an active partner in reading. There are no "right" or "wrong" answers. Accept all responses from your child and reinforce the ideas your child contributes. *(Hot cocoa is a great part of a snowy day! What other things do you like about snowy days?)*

EXPAND on this by pointing to specific objects (*What a neat fort!*) and actions (*That sled is really flying down the hill!*) and ask for your child's ideas about both "things you like" and "things you can do" related to different kinds of days.

USE your child's ideas to encourage a conversation. (*What a good idea! Having cardboard boat races on a sunny day would be lots of fun.)*

Try ECHO READING. Adult reads a small amount of text and invites the child to echo it back. (Adult: *What do you like about icy days?* Child: *What do you like about icy days?* Adult: *Sweaters and soup.* Child: *Sweaters and soup.)*

LOOK for a friendly frog. He is enjoying all the special days, too!

GET INSPIRED! Take photographs of what you do on different types of days and create your OWN story!

HAVE FUN READING TOGETHER! This is the most important thing you can do to help your child become a good reader.